THERE'S A PARTY AT MONA'S TONIGHT

BY HARRY ALLARD/ILLUSTRATED BY JAMES MARSHALL
A PICTURE YEARLING BOOK

Published by
Bantam Doubleday Dell Books for Young Readers
a division of
Bantam Doubleday Dell Publishing Group, Inc.
1540 Broadway
New York, New York 10036

ISBN: 0-440-41366-4

Book design by Julie E. Baker

Reprinted by arrangement with Doubleday Books for Young Readers

Printed in the United States of America

June 1997

10 9 8 7 6 5 4 3 2

Potter Pig was peacefully nightfishing for guppies when a cart clattered by overhead.

"There's a party at Mona's tonight!" someone shouted. Potter Pig pricked up his ears. "A party at Mona's," he said. "Hmmm." Putting his fishing pole aside, Potter rowed to shore.

He raced to Mona's on his motorcycle. "It's odd that Mona didn't invite me," he said. "Mona always invites me to her lovely parties. The mailman must have lost the invitation."

At Mona's, Potter heard laughter, music, and dancing. And he smelled delicious food.

He knocked on Mona's door. "Open up, Mona!"
he shouted. "It's me, Potter Pig."

Mona stomped to the door and yelled, "Go away, Potter Pig!" With that, she slammed the door in his face.

Potter sat down on the front step. "Mona must have mistaken me for some other Potter Pig," he said. He knocked on the door again.

This time Mona stuck her head out the window
and yelled, "Beat it, Potter!"

Then she yanked down the shade. "Strange,"
said Potter.

Potter went home and poured himself a cup of
cocoa. "I just don't understand it," he sighed.
"Doesn't Mona realize I'm always the life of
the party?"

Potter was just not going to take no for an
answer. By hook or by crook, he was going to
attend Mona's lovely party.

Later that evening, a statue was delivered to
Mona's. Mona was thrilled.

But when the statue sneezed, Mona booted it
out the door.

"Rats!" said Potter Pig, heading home. "I'll just have to think of some other way."

Fifteen minutes later, a Scottish bagpiper
appeared at the party.

"You can't fool me, Potter Pig!" yelled Mona,
and out he went, bagpipes and all.

Potter decided to tunnel his way into Mona's basement.

He said he was from the gas company and had come to read the gas meter. Mona didn't buy it. "Scram, Potter!" she said.

Potter put on his thinking cap. "I will not give up," he said, clenching his fists. "Where there's a will, there's a way!"

Potter hired a dirigible and had himself
lowered down Mona's chimney disguised as
Santa Claus.

But, since it was the middle of summer, Potter
could not bamboozle Mona. She showed him
the door.

A little while later, Potter ran into Blossom
Skunk. "I think Mona is mad at me," he said.
"But I just don't know why."
"Why don't you ask her?" suggested Blossom.

Potter dialed Mona's number. "Mona," he said,
"why are you mad at me?"
"Because you told Bruce the Toad I had big
feet!" said Mona.

"Why, Mona, I never said you had big feet,"
said Potter.
"Well, in *that* case," said Mona, "why don't you
come to my party?"

Mona greeted Potter with open arms. "We've missed you!" she said, giving him a party hat.

Potter was so glad that he had made up with
Mona. Soon, he was having the time of his life.

But while Mona was dancing a wild fandango,
Potter turned to Bruce the Toad and whispered,
"But you know, Mona *does* have big feet!"

"I heard that, Potter!" cried Mona.

And she kicked Potter out. "And don't you *dare*
come back!" she shouted.

Later that evening, a lady knocked at the door.
"I'm your aunt Gertrude, Mona," she said.
"Don't you recognize me, dear?"